Harold Shows Off

Learn to read with Thomas

EGMONT
We bring stories to life

First published in Great Britain 2008
by Egmont UK Limited
239 Kensington High Street, London W8 6SA
All rights reserved.

HiT entertainment

Thomas the Tank Engine & Friends™

CREATED BY BRITT ALLCROFT
Based on the Railway Series by the Reverend W Awdry
© 2008 Gullane (Thomas) LLC. A HIT Entertainment company.
Thomas the Tank Engine & Friends and Thomas & Friends are trademarks of Gullane (Thomas) Limited.
Thomas the Tank Engine & Friends and Design is Reg. U.S. Pat. & Tm. Off.

ISBN 978 1 4052 3790 1
1 3 5 7 9 10 8 6 4 2

Printed in Singapore

Learn to read with Thomas

This series of early learning story books draws on the 45 key words that children learn in the first year of the National Curriculum.

The stories contain repetition of these key words and phrases. This will help your child to recognise them, and to make the link between their sounds and their shapes on the page. Your child will also begin to predict what is coming next, thus connecting written and spoken words, enabling them to 'read'.

Listening to stories read aloud motivates children to want to read for themselves, and well-loved characters like Thomas encourage their interest in books.

To get the most out of the stories:

- read them with your child on several occasions;
- use a lively tone of voice and point to the words;
- encourage your child to read aloud the words he/she has learned.

Other activities to enjoy:

- **Match the pictures**
  Children can scan the page from left to right in preparation for reading and writing.

- **Find the pictures**
  Children can learn to observe small details in this activity.

- **Spot the difference**
  Children will compare two pictures, a skill used in reading when distinguishing the shapes of letters and words.

Harold is a big helicopter.

Harold says that he is better than the engines.

"I can fly," says Harold to Thomas.

"You can only go on rails," says Harold.

"Look at me," says Harold.

"I can go up and down," says Harold.

"Show me," says Thomas. "Go up and down."

Harold goes up and down.

"I can go round and round," says Harold.

"Show me," says Thomas. "Go round and round."

Harold goes round and round, up and down.

It makes Harold dizzy!

Harold goes from side to side.

It makes Harold very dizzy.

"You can't fly now," says Thomas.

"But I can go! Look at me!"

Draw a line between the pictures that are the same.

Point to these things in the big picture.

These pictures look the same, but there are
5 differences in picture 2.

Can you spot them all?

Answers: the spirals are missing from the sky, James' smoke is missing, The Fat Controller's shirt is blue, James' number 5 is missing and Harold's windows are missing.

Learn to read with Thomas

This pre-reading programme is designed to encourage an early confidence in reading. It features 40 of the frequent use-words as set out in the National Curriculum, plus key vocabulary from the Thomas Learning programme.

Read on with Thomas with the full range of titles:

Harold Shows Off
9781405237901

Really Useful Bertie
9781405237888

A Job for Donald and Douglas
9781405237895

Thomas and the Bees
9781405237871

Free Poster!

Reading with Thomas is as easy as ABC. To claim this attractive poster, log on to www.egmont.co.uk/learntoread. Offer ends 31st December 2008. Available while stocks last.

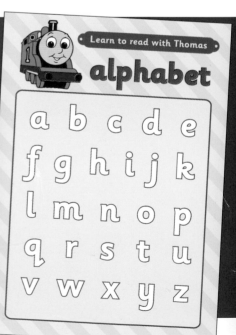

Learn with Thomas

Learn with Thomas books are designed to encourage discovery of key early learning concepts, such as logic, fine motor skills, colour, early maths, reading and language as well as inspiring parents and toddlers to interact.

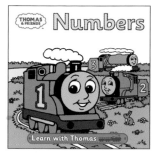

Numbers
9781405232098

Words
9781405232081

Shapes
9781405232074

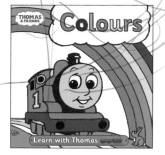

Colours
9781405232104

Clock Book
9781405238571

Opposites
9781405240611

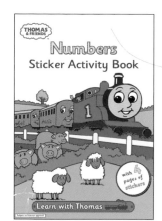

Numbers Sticker Activity
9781405239899

Words Sticker Activity
9781405239905

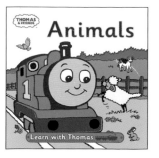

Animals
9781405240604

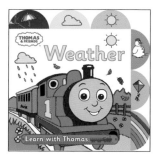

Weather
9781405240598

For more information about the Learn with Thomas range log onto www.egmont.co.uk/learnwiththomas

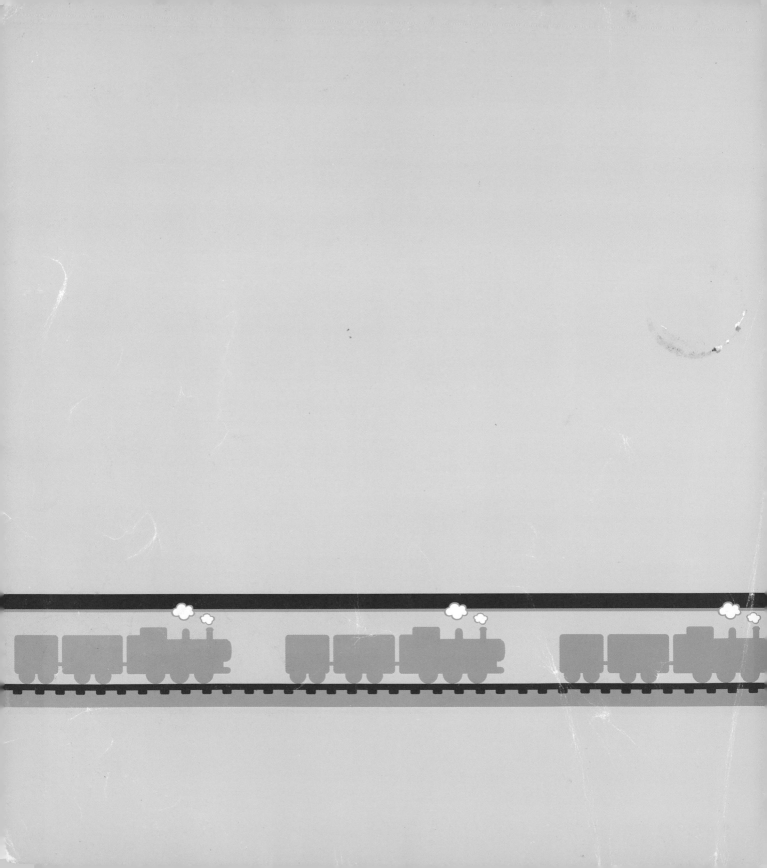